THE NITROGEN CYCLE

The Rosen Publishing Group's

PowerKids Press™

New York

Suzanne Slade

To Mr. Bill Hust, for all your hard work and dedication to the kids at Rockland School

Published in 2007 by the Rosen Publishing Group, Inc.
29 East 21st Street, New York, NY 10010

First Edition

Editor: Joanne Randolph
Book Design: Greg Tucker
Photo Researcher: Jeffrey Wendt

Illustrations: pp. 4, 5, 9, 11 by Tahara Anderson.
Photo Credits: Cover, p. 1 © Dr. Tony Brain/Photo Researchers, Inc.; p. 6 © John M. Daugherty/Photo Researchers, Inc.; p. 7 © Kenneth Eward/BioGrafx/Photo Researchers, Inc.; p. 8 © Biophoto Associates/Photo Researchers, Inc.; p. 10 © Momatiuk - Eastcott/Corbis; p. 12 © Adam Hart-Davis/Photo Researchers, Inc.; p. 13 © Pr. Courtieu/Photo Researchers, Inc.; p. 14 © Frank J. Miller/Photo Researchers, Inc.; p. 15 © Keren Su/Corbis; p. 16 © Jim Reed/Corbis; p. 17 © David Allio/Icon SMI/Corbis; p. 18 © Patrick Bennett/Corbis; p. 19 © Dr. Jeremy Burgess/Photo Researchers, Inc.; p. 20 © Reuters/Corbis; p. 21 © Michael P. Gadomski/Photo Researchers, Inc.

Library of Congress Cataloging-in-Publication Data

Slade, Suzanne.
  The nitrogen cycle / Suzanne Slade.— 1st ed.
     p. cm. — (Cycles in nature)
  Includes index.
  ISBN 1-4042-3491-8 (library binding) — ISBN 1-4042-2200-6 (pbk.) — ISBN 1-4042-2390-8 (six pack)
  1. Nitrogen—Juvenile literature. 2. Cycles—Juvenile literature. I. Title. II. Series: Cycles in nature (Rosen Pub. Group's PowerKids Press)

QD181.N1S645 2007
546'.711—dc22

                                                        2005035818

Manufactured in the United States of America

Contents

What Is Nitrogen?

There are 94 natural **elements** in the world. Elements make up every solid, liquid, and gas. Earth and the air surrounding it are made of elements, too. All living things need an element called nitrogen to stay alive. Pure nitrogen is almost always found in the form of a gas. Nitrogen gas has no color, odor, or taste.

Every element has a **symbol** of one, two, or three letters. Nitrogen's symbol is the letter *N*. Elements are made of **particles** that are too small to see called **atoms**.

A nitrogen atom has 7 electrons, which are shown as small circles with a minus sign in them. It has 7 protons, too. The protons have a plus sign in them. The number of neutrons in a nitrogen atom is not always the same.

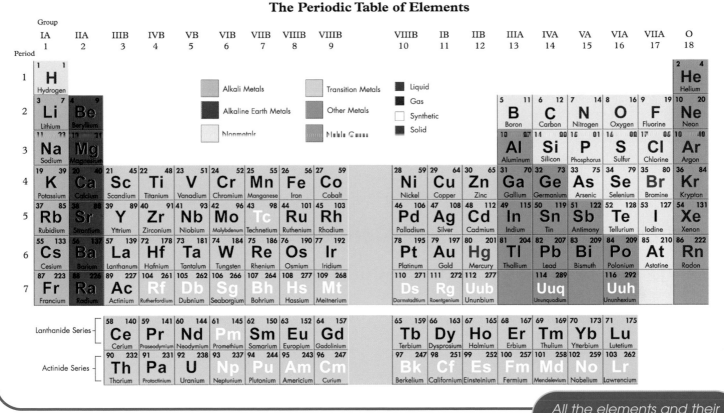

The Periodic Table of Elements

Atoms are made of three smaller particles called **protons**, **neutrons**, and **electrons**. Atoms can join together to form **molecules**. A molecule of nitrogen gas is made of two nitrogen atoms.

All the elements and their symbols are listed on a chart called the periodic table. Can you find the symbol for nitrogen here?

Cycle Facts

Atoms in a molecule are held together by forces between electrons called bonds.

Nitrogen in Living Things

Nitrogen is an important element for all living things. Animals and plants need nitrogen to live and grow. Living things use molecules with nitrogen atoms, called nitrogen compounds, every day. Compounds are made of atoms from different elements.

Our bodies need different nitrogen compounds to make many kinds of **proteins**. Proteins help build muscles. Muscles allow you to move, run, jump, and lift things. Your

Here we see shoulder, chest, and neck muscles. Muscles can contract, or get smaller. They can also get larger again. This is how we are able to move our body parts.

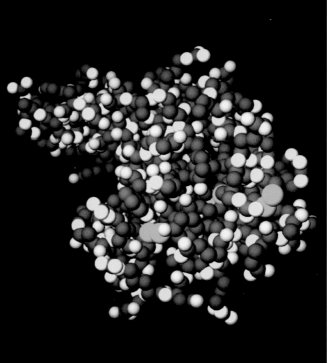

lungs and heart are made of proteins. Proteins are also found in your hair, skin, fingernails, and bones. Plants use proteins to make stems and leaves.

Proteins also make **enzymes** in your body. Every enzyme has its own special job to do. For example, an enzyme called lactase breaks down a sugar called lactose present in milk and dairy products.

An enzyme called lysozyme is found in your tears. It keeps your eyes safe from tiny living things that can cause sickness.

Cycle Facts

Nitrogen was discovered more than 200 years ago. A French scientist, Jean-Antoine Chaptal, gave nitrogen its name.

Nitrogen Moves in a Cycle

Nitrogen atoms are used again and again as they move in a **cycle** through nature. Nitrogen travels in the form of many different compounds as it moves through the air, soil, living things, and finally back into the air again.

Bacteria, living things that are too small to see without special tools, are very important in the nitrogen cycle. Bacteria in the soil take nitrogen gas from the air and make nitrogen compounds. Plants pull in these nitrogen compounds through

This is a close-up view of cyanobacteria. Cyanobacteria usually live in water and create their own food. They also live within plants' cells and let the plant make food. Cyanobacteria supply nitrogen that is used to grow beans and rice, too.

nitrogen (N_2) in the air

lightning

burning of fossil fuels puts nitrogen into the air

emissions from industrial combustion and gasoline engines

volcano

fossil fuels

bacteria take nutrients out of the soil and put it into the air

nitrogen fixing bacteria in roots

decay of dead animals and plants

nitrates (NO_3^-)

nitrogen fixing bacteria in soil

creates ammonia

fungi and bacteria (decomposers)

nitrates (NO_2^-)

ammonia (NH_3)

their roots and create new compounds. When animals eat plants, they take in the nitrogen compounds that plants created. When animals and plants die, some of their nitrogen compounds go into the earth. Other bacteria change some of the nitrogen compounds in dead plants and animals into nitrogen gas. This completes the cycle.

Cycle Facts

Over time bacteria in the soil put about the same amount of nitrogen into the air as other bacteria take from the air. This keeps the nitrogen cycle in balance.

9

Nitrogen in the Air

Every breath you take is mostly nitrogen gas. The air around you is nearly 80 **percent** nitrogen gas. Although your body needs nitrogen, it cannot use the nitrogen gas you breathe in. You breathe all of it right back out again.

Nitrogen gas is shown by the formula N_2. A formula shows how many atoms of each element are joined together in one molecule of an element or compound. The small number beside the N means there are two nitrogen atoms in one nitrogen molecule.

The air that surrounds Earth is called the atmosphere. It is filled with gases, such as nitrogen, oxygen, and water vapor. Most of the atmosphere is made of nitrogen.

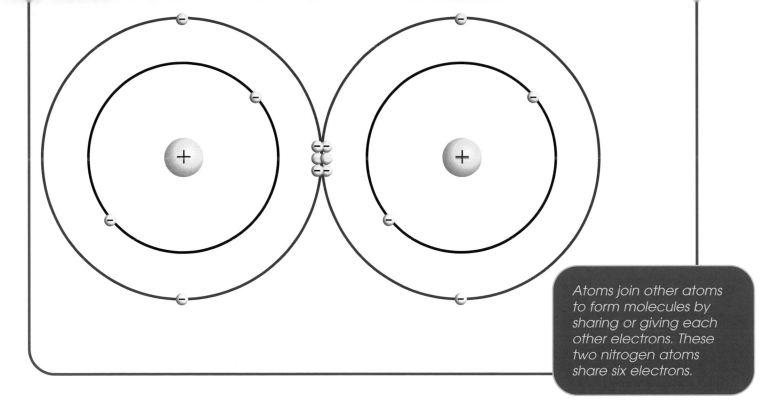

Atoms join other atoms to form molecules by sharing or giving each other electrons. These two nitrogen atoms share six electrons.

These two nitrogen atoms are held together by three **bonds**. Each of these bonds is formed by a pair of electrons shared between the nitrogen atoms. There are three bonds in a nitrogen gas molecule, so the nitrogen atoms share a total of six electrons.

Cycle Facts

Nitrogen gas is called a stable element because the three bonds that hold the two nitrogen atoms together are strong.

The simple science equation below shows how nitrogen atoms form a molecule of nitrogen gas. An equation tells you how the part on the left equals the part on the right.

$$N + N \longrightarrow N_2$$

| Nitrogen Atom | + | Nitrogen Atom | → | One Molecule of Nitrogen Gas |

Nitrogen in Plants

Plants need nitrogen to live and grow. Before plants can use nitrogen, it must be broken down into a new form. A **process** called nitrogen fixation breaks the three bonds in a nitrogen molecule. Then it changes the nitrogen into nitrogen compounds.

During nitrogen fixation bacteria in the soil use an enzyme called nitrogenase to break the bonds in nitrogen gas molecules. Then this enzyme helps the single nitrogen atoms bond with hydrogen atoms to make a compound called ammonia. Ammonia has the

This is a model of an ammonia molecule. The blue ball is a nitrogen atom. The three white balls are hydrogen atoms. The sticks that connect them stand for the bonds that join the atoms.

formula NH_3. One molecule of ammonia has one nitrogen atom and three hydrogen atoms. Hydrogen is a gas you cannot see, smell, or taste. Plants are able to take in the ammonia and use it to live and grow.

Plants also get nitrogen through a process called nitrification. In this process other bacteria in the soil change ammonia into nitrogen compounds called nitrates.

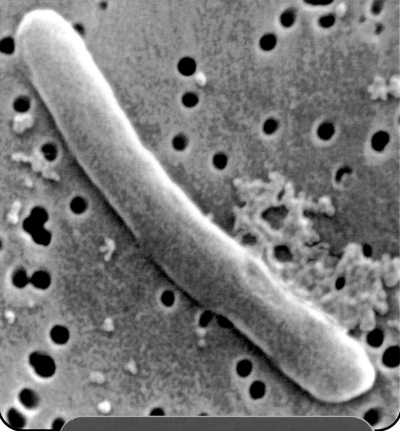

This is a close-up of a clostridium bacteria. Some kinds of clostridium are nitrogen-fixing bacteria.

Cycle Facts

There are many different nitrate compounds. No matter which elements make up the different nitrate compounds, they all have one thing in common. All nitrate compounds have one atom of nitrogen and three atoms of oxygen.

Nitrogen in Animals

The nitrogen cycle continues as animals take in nitrogen compounds by eating plants. Animals also get nitrogen by eating other animals. Animals have nitrogen stored in their bodies from eating plants and animals. For example, you get nitrogen from the meat or vegetables on your pizza. Animals need nitrogen to create proteins, which help their bodies grow and move.

When an animal dies, its body decays, or rots. When a body decays, it slowly breaks down

Mushrooms are called decomposers. This means they help dead plants and animals break down.

As this panda eats bamboo it is taking in nitrogen compounds. A panda needs to eat about 40 pounds (18 kg) of food each day.

into its basic elements. The nitrogen compounds in the proteins of an animal's body break down, too. These nitrogen compounds are turned into ammonia by bacteria in the soil. Other bacteria take some of this ammonia and change it into nitrogen compounds that plants need. Animals are a part of the nitrogen cycle as they eat, live, and die.

Cycle Facts

People get more nitrogen from plants and meat than their bodies can use. Your body gets rid of the extra nitrogen in the form of ammonia (NH_3).

Nitrogen Compounds

Bacteria are not the only producers of nitrogen compounds. Lightning changes nitrogen gas in the air into compounds that plants use, too. Lightning heats the air around it to about 60,000° F (33,000° C). This heat breaks the three bonds in a nitrogen gas molecule and creates single nitrogen atoms. Single nitrogen atoms join with **oxygen** atoms to make nitrogen monoxide gas (NO) and a gas called nitrogen dioxide (NO_2). Different processes in the soil and air

Every year lightning makes about 10 million tons (9 million t) of nitrogen compounds for plants.

A nitrogen compound called nitromethane is burned to make special cars go fast. These cars, called funny cars, can move at speeds of about 330 miles per hour (531 km/h).

change these nitrogen oxides gases into nitrogen compounds that plants need.

Besides helping plants and animals grow, nitrogen compounds are useful in many ways. Nitric acid is a nitrogen compound used to make colorful dyes for cloth. A compound called potassium nitrate helps make beautiful fireworks.

Cycle Facts

Police use a nitrogen compound called silver nitrate to find people who have been near a crime. When people touch paper, their fingers leave some oil or sweat on the paper. If that paper is sprayed with silver nitrate and put under a light, a brown fingerprint will appear. Police use fingerprints to find the people who took part in a crime.

Nitrogen and Farming

If the nitrogen cycle is left alone, it puts enough nitrogen back into the soil for plants to grow. However, people do things that have an effect on the nitrogen cycle.

Farmers grow crops in the same field year after year. They gather the plants and nothing is left to decay and feed the nitrogen-producing bacteria. Over time the plants on this piece of land take most of the nitrogen compounds out of the soil. Rain also washes some of the compounds away. To help their plants grow,

Soybeans are a kind of legume. Soy supplies the soil with nitrogen. It is also used as a food and to make many products, such as soap and paint.

some farmers add nitrogen back into the soil with **fertilizers**. Other farmers try to make sure their fields have enough nitrogen by rotating their crops. Instead of planting their usual crops, they will plant **legumes**, such as peanuts, every few years. Legumes work with certain bacteria to produce large amounts of nitrogen that help replenish, or renew, the soil.

Here you can see root nodules on the roots of a legume. The nodules, or bumps, are caused by the nitrogen-fixing bacteria Rhizobium. This bacteria provides the plant with the food it needs to live. In turn the plant supplies the bacteria with nitrogen.

Cycle Facts

Farmers also use natural compounds to fertilize their fields. Bird droppings, also called guano, are about 10 percent nitrogen. The nitrogen in guano helps crops, like corn and peanuts, grow.

Upsetting the Cycle

For millions of years, the nitrogen cycle has stayed in balance. Scientists are concerned that factories, farmers, and cars are upsetting that natural cycle. Too many nitrogen compounds in our world can hurt, not help, plants and animals.

Factories and cars create nitrogen monoxide and nitrogen dioxide gases when they burn coal, oil, and gas. Nitrogen dioxide is what makes the air in some cities smell bad and look brown. Breathing in too much nitrogen dioxide is harmful.

We call the nitrogen dioxide in the air around some cities smog. Smog is not safe for people to breathe.

When nitrogen monoxide mixes with rainwater it makes a liquid called nitric acid. Nitric acid kills fish and can destroy buildings.

This lake is filled with plants and algae. The growth of too many algae and plants can be caused by nitrogen in fertilizers.

Rainwater washes some nitrogen fertilizers into lakes. This extra nitrogen causes plants, **algae**, and other living things in lakes to grow and use the oxygen that fish need. The increase in algae can also block sunlight, which can cause plants to die. Sometimes fertilizers get in our drinking water and make it unsafe.

Cycle Facts

A black powder made of nitrogen compounds is used in some types of guns. This powder explodes when it is lit with a spark. Sticks of explosives that are filled with nitrogen compounds also explode when lit with fire.

The Nitrogen Cycle in Our World

Living things depend on the nitrogen cycle to stay alive. Nitrogen begins its cycle as pure nitrogen gas. It then continues through the cycle in the form of many different compounds.

People have discovered many helpful uses for pure nitrogen gas. Nitrogen gas is used in airplane tires because it always takes up the same amount of space, unlike other gases. Potato-chip bags are filled with nitrogen gas to keep chips fresh and protect them from breaking. Nitrogen gas changes into a liquid at -321° F (-196° C). Liquid nitrogen freezes things instantly. Fruits and vegetables are frozen with liquid nitrogen so they can be safely shipped and stored until people buy them. Doctors freeze unhealthy skin with liquid nitrogen, too. Nitrogen is a necessary and useful element for living things as it cycles through our world.

Cycle Facts

Nitrogen gas also helps save lives. Nitrogen gas fills a car air bag in less than one second, providing a soft place for people to land if they are hit by another car.

Glossary

algae (AL-jee) Plantlike living things without roots or stems that often live in water.

atoms (A-temz) The smallest parts of elements that can exist either alone or with other elements.

bonds (BONDZ) What holds two things together.

cycle (SY-kul) A course of events that happens in the same order over and over.

electrons (ih-LEK-tronz) Particles inside atoms that spin around the nucleus. They have a negative charge.

elements (EH-luh-ments) Molecules that have all the same kind of atoms.

enzymes (EN-zymz) Matter made by cells that cause changes to other matter.

fertilizers (FUR-tuh-lyz-er) Something put in soil to help crops grow.

legumes (LEH-gyoomz) Vegetables such as a peas or beans.

lungs (LUNGZ) The parts of an air-breathing animal that take in air and supply oxygen to the blood.

molecules (MAH-lih-kyoolz) Two or more atoms joined together.

neutrons (NOO-tronz) Particles with a neutral electric charge found in the nucleus of an atom.

oxygen (OK-sih-jen) A gas that has no color, taste, or odor and is necessary for people and animals to breathe.

particles (PAR-tih-kulz) Small pieces of something.

percent (pur-SENT) One part of 100.

process (PRAH-ses) A set of actions done in a certain order.

proteins (PROH-teenz) Important elements inside the cells of plants and animals.

protons (PROH-tonz) Particles with a positive electric charge found in the nucleus of an atom.

symbol (SIM-bul) The letter or letters that stand for an element.

Index

Web Sites

Due to the changing nature of Internet links, PowerKids Press has developed an online list of Web sites related to the subject of this book. This site is updated regularly. Please use this link to access the list:
www.powerkidslinks.com/cin/nitrogen/